~ Favorite Fairy Tales ~

Aladdin

Retold by Rochelle Larkin   **Illustrated by Alan Leiner**

CREATIVE CHILD PRESS
is a registered trademark of Playmore Inc.,
Publishers and Waldman Publishing Corp., New York, N.Y.

Once upon a time there was a poor boy named Aladdin. Aladdin was not a very good boy; he ran around the streets instead of helping his mother.

One day, Aladdin was with his friends, making mischief as usual.

Suddenly a strange man grabbed Aladdin's arm. "Don't you recognize me?" the man asked.

Aladdin had never seen the man before.

"Can't you see the resemblance, Aladdin?" the man asked.

"I'm your uncle."

Aladdin was confused.

"Take me home and I'll prove it," the man said.

Aladdin didn't know what to do. The man was richly dressed, not like Aladdin. And if it wasn't his uncle, how would he know Aladdin's name?

"All right," Aladdin said. "My mother will know."
The man followed Aladdin to the poor little house.

"Look who's here, mother!" Aladdin cried. "It's my uncle!"

"Surely you know me," the man said, dabbing at the corners of his eyes as though he could not stop his tears. Aladdin's mother started crying, too.

"I have come here to help you," the man said, still dabbing at his eyes. "It is all I can do for my dear brother's family."

"Aladdin has not been a very good boy," the man said.

"I will find him work with one of the merchants of the town."

But instead of bringing Aladdin to any merchants, he led him far from the city.

"Stop here," the man announced suddenly.

"But why?" Aladdin asked, looking at the empty field.

"You'll soon see," the man replied in a wicked tone and with a wicked look in his eye.

The man stamped his foot on the ground three times. Aladdin saw a small hole appear.

"Get in," the man ordered. "And when you're there, do exactly as I tell you!"

Aladdin knew they were far from town and no one could help him. The man gave him a hard push that sent him into the hole.

Aladdin crawled down the tunnel. In the dark he saw a wooden door with a round brass handle. "Is there a door?" the man shouted. "Open it quickly!" Aladdin lifted the big brass ring and the door gave way.

Aladdin couldn't believe his eyes. Piles of gems and jewels almost blinded him. He grabbed handfuls and stuffed them into his shirt.

"Do you see it?" the man called. "Do you see an old brass lamp?"

On a jutting rock, stood a dull brass oil lamp.
"Yes, I have it," Aladdin replied. He crammed more jewels
into his shirt before crawling back out.

The man grabbed for the lamp.
As Aladdin started to hand it to him, he could feel the man
push him back. He realized the man was no uncle at all, but an evil
magician who had used him
to get the lamp.

The magician pushed Aladdin again, trying to knock him down. But as he did, the earth moved suddenly, closing the tunnel and leaving Aladdin inside in the dark with the lamp.

The magician stamped and shouted for a long time. But at last he went away.

Aladdin wondered why the magician wanted the dirty old lamp. He rubbed it to see if, under the dirt, it was gold. A great rumbling filled the cave. Aladdin rubbed his eyes. A giant was standing and bowing to him.

"I am the genie of the lamp, O master," the giant said.

"All that you ask, that will I do."

"Can you get us out of here?" Aladdin asked. He closed his eyes in fright.

When Aladdin opened his eyes again, he couldn't believe what he saw. He was wrapped in the genie's arms, flying above the roofs and towers of the city.

Before Aladdin could catch his breath, he was back in his own house with his mother.

Aladdin poured the gems on a table. But he kept the lamp, with the genie safely inside, for himself.

When he was alone, he rubbed the lamp, summoning the genie. In the twinkling of an eye, Aladdin and his mother were transported to a magnificent palace. In a beautiful room, on a high shelf out of harm's way, Aladdin placed the genie's lamp.

Aladdin and his mother were more than happy in their new home, but the magician was less than pleased. He knew Aladdin had discovered the power of the lamp. He thought about how to get it back. It would not be easy, for Aladdin would never give it up.

Then he got an idea.

The next day, disguised as a merchant, the magician filled a cart with shiny new lamps. "New lamps for old! New lamps for old!" Aladdin's mother, remembering the old lamp in her son's room, took advantage of the unexpected sale.

"Oh mother," said Aladdin when he returned, "the merchant must be the evil magician in disguise!"

Aladdin knew the magician had them in his power. He paced back and forth nervously, twisting a little ring he had brought back from the cave and always wore. As he twisted it, a great red cloud filled the room. There was another genie, as like the first one as to be his twin.

"Who are you?" Aladdin asked.

"I am the genie of the ring, O master," the giant replied.

"Can you get me anything I want?" Aladdin asked.

"O yes, master," the genie answered.

"Then get me back the lamp," Aladdin said.

In a flash, Aladdin had the old lamp in his hand. He rubbed it and brought back the other genie. The genies were glad to see each other.

"I have one more task, genie of the lamp," Aladdin said. "You must destroy the evil magician so he can not do any more harm." In a twinkling the genie was gone.

Aladdin learned to use his riches and the power of his genies well. He did great good, and he lived in his palace happily ever after.